HOLLY KELLER

Cromwell's Glasses

GREENWILLOW BOOKS
NEW YORK

Copyright © 1982 by Holly Keller
All rights reserved. No part of this book
may be reproduced or utilized in any form
or by any means, electronic or mechanical,
including photocopying, recording or by
any information storage and retrieval
system, without permission in writing from
the Publisher, Greenwillow Books,
a division of William Morrow & Company, Inc.
105 Madison Avenue, New York, N.Y. 10016.
Printed in the U.S.A.   First Edition

1 2 3 4 5 6 7 8 9 10

Library of Congress Cataloging in Publication Data
Keller, Holly.   Cromwell's glasses.
Summary: Cromwell the rabbit is clumsy
and slow until he gets glasses.
[1. Rabbits—Fiction.   2. Eyeglasses—
Fiction]   I. Title.
PZ7.K28132Cr   [E]   81-6644
ISBN 0-688-00834-8   AACR2
ISBN 0-688-00835-6 (lib. bdg.)

FOR BARRY

Even though he looked like all the other rabbits, Cromwell was different.

"He's terribly nearsighted," the doctor explained,
and it wasn't long before Cromwell knew what that meant.

He tried to play with his sisters and brother, but he
got lost so many times Mama wouldn't let him go anymore.

He was always stumbling over things.

"You're a pain," Lydia snapped when Mama left the room.

He tried his best to be helpful,
but something always went wrong.

"You've ruined our cereal, rattlebrain!"
Cynthia grumbled.

When Martin got his kite stuck in a tree and Cromwell thought it was a bird, Cynthia laughed and laughed.

Cromwell kicked her foot as hard as he could.

"Be patient," Mama said when she tucked him
  into bed that night.
"Soon you will be big enough to have eyeglasses."

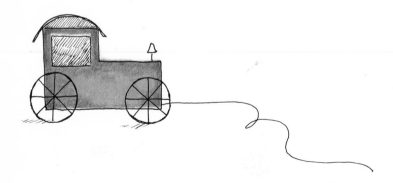

When the day finally arrived, Cromwell wasn't sure
he wanted to go to the eye doctor.
Mama gave him a new doll to help him feel brave.

The examination took a long time.

In a few days Cromwell's glasses were ready.
When he put them on, he could see much better.

He could even help Mama in the supermarket.

"He looks like an owl with big ears,"
  Lydia whispered loudly.
"More like a robot," Cynthia said, giggling.
"Awful," Martin agreed.

Cromwell thought he hated his new glasses
even more than he hated not being able to see.

The next day Mama told the children to take Cromwell
to the playground.
"Why do *we* have to get stuck with him?" Martin grumbled.

"Look at those crazy goggles!"
someone shouted when they got there.

Martin didn't know what to do.
Lydia wished she had stayed home.

Cynthia looked at Cromwell sitting by himself
in the wagon, and suddenly she felt MAD.
"Wait a minute!" she shouted.
"You can't talk about my brother like that!"

She marched over to Cromwell.
"Come on," she said, "let's play."

Cromwell followed her carefully up and down the jungle gym, and he missed only one rung. Lydia applauded.

Martin let him play marbles
and he hit a shiny red one on the second try.

He didn't miss the ball once playing catch,

and he got all the way to 4 at hopscotch.

"I think your glasses are going to be okay,"
Cynthia said when it was time to leave.
"Uh huh," Cromwell agreed.

And he slept all the way home.